Conversations With My Characters

Conversations With My Characters

By

Tracy Wilson

http://beautifulpublications.com

Published by
Beautiful Publications LLC
Stratford, CT 06614

LIBRARY OF CONGRESS CONTROL NUMBER:
2022916192
HARDCOVER ISBN: 9798-9855290-3-6
PAPERBACK ISBN: 979-8-9855290-9-8
EBOOK ISBN: 979-8-9855290-8-1

Printed in the United States of America

Contents

Dedication
Preface
Thank You
Prologue

DEDICATION

This book is dedicated to all the writers that have conversations with their characters – especially when you wish they'd shut up so you can get some sleep!

Preface

I fell in love with this cover as soon as I saw it. I think it was only on his page for two minutes before I claimed it! I was drawn to the woman looking at herself in the mirror because she was looking at her reflection.

When we look at ourselves in mirrors, we don't just see our outward appearance. We see our emotions from being groggy from waking up to being happy in the moment, confident, stressed, depressed, anxious, excited, determined, regretful, or dreadful. Applying make-up doesn't hide these emotions, but we do. It's easy to walk away from the mirror when we're feeling happy and confident but when we're not feeling so good, we leave those emotions in the mirror, put on our brave face, and head out to start our day.

Our characters are mirrors into our minds. Each character we create is another facet of our personality that we're not afraid to show our readers. People that are close to us actually read what the characters are saying in our voice because we've gotten into their head, but people that don't know us begin to wonder how much truth there is to what they see in the mirrors.

THANK YOU

Thank you Tara Gandhi-Brown for sharing Kornelia Blackmore's conversation with one of her male characters.   After reading that status I commented, "Oh – I'd like to try this!" and she responded, "You should do it - I'd be interested to see what you come up with."   My first conversation was with my character Rashad, which was published in 'His Best Friend' in March of 2021. I'd never done that before and after reading the conversation I had with him, I decided I wanted to create more conversations with more characters.

PROLOGUE

"Here we go again..." I sighed... Every time I put things in order, my characters start their shit..."

"Oh no you're not!"
"I'm tired of waiting!"
"I'm not going to shut up until you write me!"
"Don't you dare ignore me!"
"I'm talking to you!"
"I don't care who was here before me!"
"Guess who's not sleeping tonight?"
"Oh – did I wake you?"

CONVERSATION WITH BABY FROM

"Hi Baby..." I sighed as I held her...

"Is my name Baby?" she asked as she looked up at me...

"No..."

"What's my name then?"

"That's up to your parents..."

"My parents say I'm their Christmas Miracle..."

"You are their Christmas Miracle..."

"I know I'm their Christmas Miracle – but I want a name..."

"I'm pretty sure they have a name for you..."

"What if I don't like my name?"

"You'll like your name..."

"What if I don't? Can I change it?"

"You can change it when you grow up..."

"That's a long time..."

"I have an idea..."

"What's your idea?"

"If you don't like what they call you, cry until they call you something else..."

"I don't wanna cry – I wanna be happy..."

"I want you to be happy too..."

"Does anybody ever change their name?"

"Lots of people change their names..."

"Do they change their names because they don't like them?"

"Your mother changed her name when she got married..."

"She did? Why?"

"She changed her name because she loves your father..."

"I love my father too – can I have his name?"

"You'll have his last name..."

"So Me, Mommy, and Daddy all have the same last name?"

"Yes..." I got scared when she started crying... "Aww... don't cry... It's okay..."

"I'm crying because I'm happy..."

"You're happy?"

"Yea..."

"Good..."

"Can I ask you another question?"

"Sure..."

"Will I have my own room when I'm born?"

"I think so – why are you asking?"

"Well... Please don't get mad..."

"Why would I get mad at you?"

"Well... I hope I have my own room because... Never mind..."

"What's wrong?"

"I love Mommy and Daddy – but they're so loud!" I bust out laughing...

"It's not funny! Sometimes I can't go back to sleep!"

"After you're born that won't be a problem..."

"Really?"

"Really..."

"Good – 'cause I wanna be happy..."

"You'll be happy – once you go to sleep, you'll sleep like a baby..."

"How does a baby sleep?"

"They sleep until it's time to get up – unless they're hungry..."

"Will eat before I go to sleep?"

"Yes - but you might wake up if you get hungry..."

"I hope it's easy for me to go back to sleep..."

"It's easy to go back to sleep after you've been born – especially if you have your own room..."

"I hope I have my own room – 'cause I wanna be a happy baby!" she exclaimed...

"I'm sure you'll have your own room – 'cause your parents want you to be a happy baby too..."

"Really?"

"Really..."

"I'm getting tired..." she yawned...

"You can go to sleep if you want..."

"Okay..." she sighed as she nodded off in my arms.

CONVERSATION WITH BAZIL FROM
'Twisted Beautiee'

"Hello Beautiee – I mean Tracy..." he laughed...

"Hello Bazil – come in." Bazil stopped to look at our wedding photos for a few moments and then he spoke...

"I can see the resemblance..."

"I knew you would." We went to sit down on the loveseat, sat down, and just looked at each other...

"This is so weird..." he laughed...

"Are you uncomfortable?"

"Honestly?"

"Yes..."

"No – it's still weird though..."

"Why is it weird?"

"I'm looking at you... and all I can see is my wife..."

"That's good..."

"That doesn't bother you?"

"Not at all..."

"How are you okay with me telling you that I look at you and all I can see is my wife?"

"I'm okay with it because that's how I created you..."

"Yes you did..."

"And I created her too..."

"Yes you did..."

"And you love her..."

"I sure do..."

"So what would you like to know?"

"What made you write our death?"

"I didn't know I was going to write that until I got there..."

"So you didn't plot that in advance?"

"No..."

"Oh wow – I'm impressed..."

"Thank you..."

"Can I ask you a personal question?"

"Sure..."

"Have you ever... Ummm..."

"We don't invite other people into our marriage..."

"After what happened to me – I understand – but you gave us another chance..."

"Yes I did – I thought you earned a do-over..."

"Thank you..."

"You're welcome..."

"I love how you continued our story in your other books..."

"I think the readers love it too..."

"Are you finished with us?"

"Absolutely not." Bazil smiled to himself...

"I can't wait to read what happens next..."

"I can't wait to write it..."

"I love the song you wrote for us..."

"I love it too..."

"We still sing that song to each other..."

"Aww..."

"Do you think you'll write anymore songs for us?"

"I don't know..."

"You don't know or you don't want to tell me?"

"I really don't know..." I laughed...

"What about the kids?"

"Bazil?"

"Yes?"

"You're going to have to wait and see..."

"Can I get a hint?"

"No..."

"May I ask why?"

"Because I don't need you to help me write your story." Bazil smiled to himself... "Why are you smiling?"

"I'm smiling because you just answered my question..." he answered as he stood up. I stood up beside him and he smiled again...

"Why do I get the feeling you're up to something?" Bazil didn't answer me – he gave me a kiss on the cheek, walked over to the front door, opened it, turned back to wink me, and then he walked out the door and closed it behind him.

CONVERSATION WITH
BAZIL & LYDIA

The Grandparents from
'Bazil & Lydia Osgood'

"Honey – I need your help!" I exclaimed. My husband hurried into the kitchen...

"What happened?!"

"Nothing – I need you to open the door for me..."

"Put down the drinks – I'll take the drinks – you open the door..."

"Thanks..." I said as I opened the door...

"Who's coming today?"

"The Osgoods!!"

"You mean my father?" he laughed...

"Yea..." I laughed...

"Why do you always say look – your father – but you never say look – your mother?"

"Because your father is the only one I see in the commercials..."

"Do you think they all do commercials?" he asked as he put the drinks on the table...

"I've only seen one other character do commercials..."

"Let me get these other drinks..." he said as he went back in the kitchen...

"I hope they like ice tea..."

"You can't go wrong with ice tea..." he said as he put the other drinks on the table...

"Hello..." they both said in unison as they walked into the backyard...

"Hiiii!!" I exclaimed as I hugged them both...

"It's nice to meet you..." Lydia said...

"You must be our son..." Bazil said as he extended his hand to shake my husband's hand...

"I'm Gene..."

"Nice to meet you..."

"Can I have a hug?" Lydia asked...

"Sure..." my husband answered as he hugged Lydia...

"I can definitely see the resemblance..." Bazil said as we all sat down at the table and started drinking...

"My wife started telling me – look – your father – every time she saw your commercial..." my husband laughed...

"You see me in the commercial?"

"All the time!" I exclaimed...

"Do you see any of your other characters in commercials?" Lydia asked...

"We see your granddaughter..." my husband answered...

"Really?! You've seen Starr in commercials?!" Lydia exclaimed...

"Yes – we actually saw her first..." I answered...

"Aww..." Lydia sighed...

"I loved the way you brought us back from the dead..." Bazil said...

"You did?" my husband asked...

"We loved it – we laughed our asses off – what was left of them anyway..." Lydia said...

"I love how we showed up in the backyard – I was a little shocked when you had us show up outside our grandson's window instead of our son's window..." Bazil said...

"We couldn't see – we had dirt in our eyes – remember?" Lydia asked as we all bust out laughing...

"That dirt didn't get in the way when you put my dick in your mouth!" Bazil laughed...

"Bazil!!" Lydia exclaimed...

"They know – she wrote it!!" Bazil exclaimed as we all laughed...

"Does your wife show you what she writes?" Lydia asked...

"Oh yea..." my husband answered...

"Are we the craziest characters your wife has come up with?"

"Your story is kinda crazy..." he answered...

"I laughed so hard when Beautiee said really – you're asking me why I let your son watch you argue with zombies?" Lydia said...

"I used that as the synopsis on the back of my book..." I said...

"Oh my God really?"

"Oh yea..." I acknowledged...

"Thank you for helping me kill that muthafucka that was coming for my wife!" Bazil exclaimed...

"Yes – thank you!!" Lydia exclaimed...

"You're welcome – I loved writing that part!!" I exclaimed...

"I love that Beautiee wasn't afraid of us..." Lydia said...

"She had no reason to be afraid of you once she found out who you were..."

"I love that you let Beautiee publish our story from our point of view..." Bazil said...

"I felt your son needed that..."

"Will our grandchildren ever read our story?" Lydia asked...

"Well – they already know your story – especially Jay – and it was in the media..."

"That's true..." Bazil added...

"Yes – but when they get older..." Lydia started to say...

"I think our son will make sure they don't read it until they're old enough..." Bazil interrupted...

"Oh please – Jay's already explaining that Mommy & Daddy play and that's how the baby gets in Mommy's tummy..." Lydia said...

"You read that?" I asked...

"I sure did!" Lydia exclaimed...

"What can I say – like father... like son... like grandson!!" Bazil laughed...

"Oh my God!!" Lydia exclaimed...

"You know who you married!!" he laughed...

"I know exactly who I married..." she sighed as she pulled Bazil into a kiss...

"Alright now – don't start..." Bazil laughed...

"Do you act like us?" Lydia asked...

"Oh yea..." my husband laughed...

"So we get it honest..." she laughed...

"Absolutely..." my husband confirmed...

"Okay – I have to ask – are we coming back from the dead again – or are we going to stay dead?" Bazil waited for me to answer...

"Where are you going?" my husband asked as I got up...

"I'll be right back..." I answered as I went inside...

"Is she upset?" Lydia asked...

"No..." my husband answered as I came back to the table...

"Here..." I said as I handed the tablet to Bazil. His eyes got really wide as he smiled...

"Oh my God!! Tell me!!" Lydia exclaimed...

"Here..." Bazil said as he handed the tablet to Lydia...

"Oh my God!! We're going to the U.K.!!"

"How'd you come up with this?" Bazil asked...

"How much time do you have?"

"We have all eternity!!" Lydia exclaimed...

"Honey – come inside with me..." I said as I got up...

"Okay..."

"Why'd you wanna come inside?"

"We need more drinks..."

"I'll get the ice tea..."

"I'm making margaritas..." I said as I got the Dailys out of the freezer...

"I think Bazil might want something stronger..."

"I got him covered – get the Hennessey out the cabinet..."

"Okay – got it..."

"I'll put the margaritas in these glasses..."

"How do I make the Hennessey?"

"Put some ice in a glass and pour the Hennessey over it..."

"Got it." My husband got two glasses, filled them with ice, poured Hennessey in one of them, got a can of ginger ale, poured that in the other glass, and went to take them outside...

"You need any help?"

"I got it..." he answered as he put the glasses on the table, opened the door, picked up the glasses, and went back outside...

"How'd you know?" Bazil asked as my husband put the glass in front of him...

"His wife wrote the book..." Lydia answered as I set the glasses on the table, closed the door, and sat down...

"On March 20th I received a message in messenger from Claire Birkin. She volunteers with a local mental health charity and runs a book group for them named 'Tales on Tuesday' and she invited me to come speak to the group via zoom. I accepted her invite and she scheduled me for April 26th. I attended the meeting, talked about my books, and joined their Facebook group. Before the meeting ended, I told them that I write my friends into my books, I asked if anyone in the group would like to be written into a book, and John Kirkham said he'd like to become an Erotic Zombie..."

"What?!" they both exclaimed...

"Yes – I remembered Jay Covers had that cover on his website so I bought it..."

"Jay Covers? Isn't that the guy Beautiee hired to do our book cover?" Bazil asked...

"That's him..."

"So he really exists?"

"Yes..."

"Does he know you wrote him into our story?"

"Yes..."

"Well after seeing our cover and the other cover, I can see why..." Lydia said...

"On June 20th, I received an invitation to attend the 'Tales on Tuesday Awards Evening' on July 19th via zoom..."

"Oh wow..." Lydia said...

"All the authors that were invited to attend received an award – I'll show you mine..." I said as I pulled up the video on my phone and handed it to Bazil...

"Oh wow!!" Bazil exclaimed...

"Bazil!! Le'me see!!" Lydia exclaimed...

"Here..." he laughed as he handed her my phone...

"Oh my God!! It's me!!"

"It's you..." Bazil said as he pulled her into a kiss...

"They're going to put that cover on the front and the Tales on Tuesday Logo on the back of my award..."

"Oh my God – when are you going to get the award?!" Lydia exclaimed...

"I'll have it in a few weeks..."

"I wish we could see it..." she sighed...

"You will..."

"How?"

"I'll post it on my page..."

"Who made the video?" Bazil asked...

"John Kirkham..."

"Did they play this video in the ceremony?"

"They played all the videos..."

"Congratulations for winning the 'Twisted Yet Sweet' Category..."

"Thank you..."

"How does it feel to be an International Best-Selling Author?" Lydia asked...

"It feels wonderful..." I sighed as I took my husband's hand...

"Have you started writing this yet?"

"I don't need either one of you to help me write your story..." I laughed.

CONVERSATION WITH BEAUTIEE FROM

'In The Arms Of A Gangster' Beautiee's Biography

"Hiii!!" we both exclaimed as we hugged...

"This is crazy!" Beautiee laughed...

"Let's go outside..."

"Okay..." Beautiee said as she followed me outside into the backyard...

"I wanna sit in the swing!" Beautiee exclaimed...

"I know..." I said as we went over to the swing, sat down, and started swinging...

"So am I Beautiee Tracy Wilson, Beautiee in Twitter, Beautiee_Wilson in Instagram, Beautiee in Clubhouse, or DJ Beautiee?"

"You're Bazil's wife..."

"I know I'm Bazil's wife – but I'm also you..."

"You're a part of me – but you're not me..."

18

"Do you really think readers see us separately?"

"I think so..."

"What if they don't?"

"That's fine too..."

"You gave me two series..."

"Yes I did..."

"What made you do that?"

"You went through a lot in 'Twisted Beautiee'..."

"I sure did..."

"When you went to prison, you didn't know what was happening on the outside..."

"That's true – but your readers knew what was happening..."

"My readers knew what was happening, but the characters in 'Twisted Beautiee' didn't know what was happening to Beautiee – they only knew what Beautiee told them..."

"The story within the story..."

"Exactly..."

"You wanted your readers to know my story from inside..."

"I didn't just want my readers to know your story – I wanted your readers to know your story..."

"The story... within the story... within the story..."

"Exactly..."

"I love my cover..."

"I snatched it up as soon as I saw it..."

"It's perfect..."

"I'm glad you like it..."

"I love the way our story continues from the 'Twisted Series' into your other books..."

"So do I – especially when you and Bazil are the publishers of their stories!"

"Yes!! I loved it when you wrote that we were going to publish Bazil's parents' story and Jade's story!!"

"You know that Bitch had the nerve to be mad at me?"

"For what?!"

"She had the nerve to ask me why I didn't kill her..."

"Well damn – did she wanna die?!"

"She didn't wanna die – but she should've..."

"Oh my God – why?! What did she do?!"

"You're the one that's publishing her story – you tell me!!" I laughed...

"I don't know what she did yet..."

"Well... you can read 'Obsidian Heart'... you can ask her what she did... or both..."

"Ooohhh!! Your side, their side, and her side!!"

"I'm sure your readers will love her story..."

"Are we going to publish any other stories told by your characters?"

"That's a strong possibility..."

"Yes!! I knew it!! Which one?!"

"I don't know yet..."

"Our story isn't ever going to end – is it?"

"Nice try Beautiee..." I laughed...

"What'd I say?"

"Bazil tried to get me to tell him what happens next too..."

"We both know you're not done with us so why can't you tell me?"

"Like I told Bazil – I don't need you to help me write your story..."

"I know what I'm gonna do..."

"What?"

"I'm gonna read all your books and see which characters need their stories told – and when you're ready for me to tell their stories, I'll cross them off my list one by one!!" I didn't say anything. I just sat there smiling...

"Oh my God!!" she exclaimed as she jumped up...

"What's wrong?!"

"I gotta go – I just answered my question!!" she exclaimed as she hurried down the driveway and disappeared.

CONVERSATION WITH DARIEN FROM

'Caught In The Middle'

"Hello Darien..." I greeted as I opened the door. Darien just stood there... "Change your mind?"

"No..." he answered as he came inside...

"Would you rather go for a walk?"

"Why would I go for a walk when I have a car?"

"You seem anxious..."

"Is it that obvious?"

"Yes..."

"Sorry about that..."

"You want a drink?"

"You don't have anything strong enough..."

"I got Henny..."

"I'll take that..."

"On the rocks or straight up?"

"On the rocks..."

"Why don't you go sit on the deck – I can bring you your drink and we can talk outside?"

"That sounds good..." he said as he followed me into the kitchen...

"The door to the deck is..."

"I'll wait..." he interrupted...

"Le'me hurry up with the drink – you really need it!" I laughed...

"I'm sorry – I'll go outside..." he laughed as he left the kitchen, opened the door, and went outside...

"Hey..." my husband announced as he came in...

"Hey..." I sighed as I pulled him into a kiss...

"Whose car is in the driveway?"

"Darien's'..."

"Where is he?"

"He's on the deck..."

"Is that his drink or yours?"

"His..."

"I'll take it to him and introduce myself..." he said as he took the drink and went outside. I made two glasses of ice tea and took them to the door...

"Honey – could you get the door for me?"

"Sure..." he answered as he opened the door. I put the drinks on the table and sat down...

"You finish your drink already?" I asked Darien...

"Yea..."

"You want another one?"

"Naa – I need to be able to drive..."

"Okay... I guess we can get started..."

"I can't believe I didn't shoot that muthafucka..." he laughed...

"That would've been a different story..."

"Oh so when you came up with the title 'Caught In The Middle' you meant that literally!!" he laughed...

"Yes..."

"Did you read the first few pages?" he asked as he turned to my husband...

"Oh yea..."

"What would you have done?"

"I would 'a caught a charge..."

"See?! Why couldn't I catch a charge?!"

"Because he didn't deserve Lacey..."

"He wasn't going to get Lacey anyway!!"

"Who do you think she would've turned to if you went to prison?"

"Well... Dexter would've been dead so..."

"So it would've been another man..."

"I guess..."

"I didn't want her to turn to another man – I wanted her to face what she did... and why..."

"You made me look like a fool..." My husband's eyes got really big. I thought he was going to say something...

"I knew it..."

"You knew what?"

"I knew that's how you felt..."

"Why didn't you let me kill him?!"

"You don't like the way he died?"

"I love that he's dead – I just wanted to be the one to do it..."

"I couldn't let you kill him... or her..."

"I wasn't going to kill Lacey..."

"As angry as you were... you don't know what you were capable of – but I did – and I had to make sure your marriage survived..."

"I'm glad our marriage survived..."

"So am I..."

"Now – about that visit to the doctor..."

"That was crazy!!" I laughed...

"I'm glad you were amused!!"

"Oh c'mon – you don't think the readers eyes were glued to that chapter?"

"I bet they were!! I was wondering what you were going to have him do to me!!"

"It turned out okay didn't it?"

"That's not the point..."

"Of course it is..."

"So can I relax or do you have other plans for us?"

"I wasn't planning on doing anything else with you but that can always change..."

"Damn – I should 'a kept my mouth shut!!" he laughed...

"You know... now that you mention it... I could..."

"Don't you dare!!" he laughed...

"What if the readers want more?" Darien sat there deep in thought for a few moments...

"Tell you what – if you want to bring in another woman for me – that'll work..."

"I see you startin' a feel that Henny..." I laughed...

"Le'me go..." he said as he got up to leave...

"You sure you don't want another drink?"

"Naa... I need to get home to Lacey..."

"Are you going to tell her you want another woman?"

"Hell no!!" he laughed as he got in his car, started it, and drove off.

CONVERSATION WITH HELEN FROM

Helen

Helen & Harmony Series

"Hello Helen..." I greeted as I opened the door. Helen didn't speak. She just walked in and went to sit on the loveseat. I went over to the loveseat and sat down beside her... "This isn't going to work unless you speak to me..."

"Maybe this wasn't such a good idea after all..." she said as she stood up and walked towards the door...

"That's fine – it was nice seeing you – tell Rashad I said hello..."

"Oh hell no!" she laughed as she came back over to the loveseat and sat down...

"What happened between you and Rashad?"

"This isn't about Rashad..."

"You were ready to walk out the door – but it wasn't about Rashad? Yea – okay..."

"You have any coffee?"

"I have coffee..." I answered as I got up and went into the kitchen... "Come sit in the dining room..."

"Okay..." she said as she got up. I noticed her smiling as she went into the dining room and sat at the table... "You have any creamer?" I stopped to look at her and went back to making the coffee. When I was finished, I put a cup in front of her and sat down... "Hazelenut..."

"How'd you know?"

"I can smell it..." she answered before she took a sip..."

"So what happened between you and Rashad?"

"Not a damn thing!!" she laughed...

"Really?! Why?!"

"If I wanted a child to play with you would've found me one..."

"What's that supposed to mean?!"

"Ain't nobody got time for no immature, game-runnin', corny-ass Rashad!!" she laughed...

"That bad huh?"

"He would've done better if he just wanted to hit it and quit it..."

"Wow..."

"Oh please – don't act so surprised – you know I wasn't craving dick like that..."

"You weren't craving dick, but you were craving love..."

"Now see – we were getting along so nice – why'd you have to go and say that?"

"Because that's the reason you didn't want to speak to me..."

"You still didn't have to say it..."

"I think I did..."

"Why?"

"When I started posting 'Helen' I got a few comments from readers that had a mother-in-law like you..."

"So their mother-in-law's were crazy?"

"Sometimes there's a reason behind the madness..."

"Sometimes there isn't..."

"There was a reason behind your madness..."

"You still made me look crazy!!"

"I didn't make you look crazy – I explained your crazy..."

"People don't give a shit about that..."

"Yes they do..."

"Yea right..."

"They do..."

"You're just saying that to justify how you created me..."

"Before I wrote your story I saw a lot of posts in social media about people dealing with a toxic mother-in-law..."

"So now you're saying I was crazy and toxic – you know what – I don't have to put up with this shit – I can leave!!" she exclaimed as she got up...

"You could leave... or you could sit back down and be mad at me..."

"Why would you want me to sit back down and be mad at you?!"

"I'm willing to do whatever it takes to finish this conversation..."

"Okay – since you wanna have this conversation – have you ever been in a relationship where you had to deal with a crazy, psychotic, or toxic person?"

"No I haven't..."

"So Harmony isn't based on a true story?"

"Harmony is based on those readers that can identify with her because they're going through it..."

"What about me?"

"I don't understand your question..."

"Did you really have to make me put on a dildo, take a video, and post it to Facebook?!"

"No - I didn't have to do that..."

"I don't hear an apology..."

"Is that why you're still here?!"

"You don't think you owe me an apology?!"

"I didn't invite you here to apologize..." I laughed...

"Well why the fuck did you invite me here then?!"

"I invited you here to give you an opportunity to say what's on your mind..."

30

"Thanks for wasting my time!!" she exclaimed as she jumped up from the table, stormed through the kitchen and living room, flung the door open, stormed out, and slammed the door behind her...

"Bitch really thought I was apologizing!" I laughed.

CONVERSATION WITH
HORACE FROM
Harmony'
Helen & Harmony Series

"Hello Horace..." I greeted as I opened the door...

"Hello Tracy..." he greeted as he came inside...

"Let's sit..."

"Okay." Horace followed me over to the sofa and we both sat down...

"Where would you like to start?"

"Did you really have to kill me?"

"Yes..."

"Killing my mother wasn't enough?"

"No..."

"Why not?!"

"Wait a minute – are you actually saying you would've been okay with me killing your mother if I had let you live?!"

"I didn't want her to die either – I'm just sayin' – did you kill a mother and son in any of your other books?"

"So far... no..."

"See?!"

"I'm sorry you're upset – but your story kinda wrote itself..."

"What's that supposed to mean?!"

"Well – look at what you did to your brother..."

"You talkin' about that shit in high school?"

"Yes..."

"Man – we were kids – he should 'a let that go a long time ago!!"

"That's easy for you to say..."

"If the situation were in reverse – I would 'a let that shit go!!"

"No you wouldn't..."

"How you gon' tell me?!"

"I know you – I created you..."

"So what – I would 'a killed my brother?!"

"Yes..."

"You just wanted somebody else to die..."

"Actually... I wasn't planning to kill you in the beginning..."

"You didn't plan it?!"

"No..."

"So what – it just happened?!"

"Basically..."

"You're full of shit!!"

"No I'm not..."

"When did you decide to kill me then?"

"I decided to kill you after you and Harmony met at the hotel..."

"Why?! That was consensual!!"

"You know I wrote the book – right?"

"Whatever..."

"Would you have let your brother get away with that – again?"

"What are you talkin' about – it only happened once!!"

"It happened twice..."

"What are you talkin' about?!"

"You know exactly what I'm talkin' about..."

"My mother was right about you..."

"You and your mother are a lot alike..."

"Don't talk about my mother!!"

"Classic narcissist..."

"Narcissist?!"

"You don't like what I'm saying so you're deflecting..."

"So what – I'm supposed to be happy you killed me?!"

"You're not happy I killed you – I get that – but you're angry because you asked me a question, I answered it, and you don't like my answer..."

"Of course I don't like your answer – you could've let me live!!" I sat there quiet for a few moments just looking at Horace before I spoke...

"I get it..." I said as I smiled...

"You get it?! Then why are you smiling?!"

"You're not mad because I killed your mother and you're not mad because I killed you – you're mad because you didn't get the girl..."

"Harmony?! I didn't want her!!"

"Yes you did..."

"Yea right!!"

"I'm right – aren't I?"

"I didn't want Harmony!!"

"You wanted to beat your brother..."

"It wasn't a race!!"

"You're here because you're angry – you're angry because you didn't want to die – you're angry because you wanted to live – and you wanted to live with Harmony..."

"I didn't want my brother's girl..."

"You wanted your brother's life – and if you were allowed to live – you would've made his life a living hell trying to take it..."

"You know what – I don't have to sit here and listen to this shit – I can leave!!" he exclaimed as he jumped up...

"I didn't stop your mother from leaving... and I'm not stopping you..."

"FUCK YOU!!" he exclaimed as he went over to the door, flung it open, stormed out, and ran smack into my husband...

"Hello Horace..." my husband greeted...

"Good bye!!" he exclaimed as he stepped around my husband and stormed down the street...

"Hey..." my husband sighed as he came in...

"Hey..." I sighed as I got up and went to greet him...

"You okay?" he asked as he pulled me into a hug...

"I'm okay..."

"You sure you're alright?" he asked as he continued to hold me...

"Yea...." I sighed...

"I should've been here..."

"I'm glad you weren't here..."

"Really?!"

"Yea..."

"Why?"

"Because if you were here, he wouldn't've spoken his truth."

CONVERSATION WITH JADE FROM

'Obsidian Heart'

"Hello..." I greeted as I opened the door for Jade...

"Thank you for agreeing to speak to me..." Jade said...

"You're welcome – let's go sit out on the deck..."

"Wow - you have a nice collection of crystals..."

"Thank you..."

"I'm beginning to understand why you wrote Obsidian's story..." she said as she followed me into the dining room...

"It's not just his story – it's our story..." I said as I opened the door to the deck and we went to sit outside...

"True – but I'm not here to talk about Sid – I'm here to talk about you... and me..."

"Why'd you want to speak to me?" I asked, as if I didn't already know the answer...

"You know damn well why I wanted to speak to you!" she snapped...

"Watch your tone Jade..."

"Oh – that's right – you like to kill your characters..." she said as she rolled her eyes...

"Keep that up and I'll write a part 3 and your happy ending won't be so happy..."

"I'm sorry Tracy – I didn't mean it like that..."

"Apology accepted..."

"Thank you – I'm here because I don't understand why you didn't kill me – especially when I killed you in a past life and tried to kill you in this one..."

"I never had any intention of killing you – my intent was to tell a drama filled story of crystals, gemstones, spheres, psychics, past lives, and chakras. I started the story with the intent to write my friend Chris and her wife into it – but after I did the readings and discovered that our lives ended tragically, I had to mix it up, create drama, and keep my readers on the edge of their seats..."

"I still don't get why you didn't kill me..."

"Well damn – did you really wanna die?" I laughed...

"Of course not – I just figured that's where you'd go – it's not like I didn't deserve to die – I did try and kill you - again..." she laughed...

"Yes you did – but I wanted my readers to understand what you were feeling..."

"Especially since you stole my husband's heart..." she laughed...

"He was husband first!" I laughed...

"Yes - he was your husband in a past life – and now he's your husband in this life..."

"Yes he is..." I sighed...

"Why'd you give me a happy ending? Why didn't you let me rot in prison?"

"You'll do your time – but I felt you deserved another chance to be happy – if I didn't come back to drop off the key you wouldn't've tried to kill me..."

"I thought your friend Chris said you were supposed to be there?"

"I was – but what if I waited until the next day?"

"Then I might've gotten out in 7 years instead of 12..." she sighed...

"Exactly..."

"Are you going to write a part 3 and let everyone see us living happily ever after?"

"No..."

"Okay..." she laughed... "I tried it - thanks for not killing me..." she said as she got up...

"How's your husband?"

"He's as good as you can get in prison..." she laughed...

"Good..."

"Alright – I'll see myself out..." she said as she got up...

"I'll let you out..." I said...

"Relax – it's a nice day – I'll walk..." she said as she walked through the backyard, down the driveway, and then she disappeared.

CONVERSATION WITH JERMOLL FROM 'Erotic Zombies'

"Hello Jermoll..." I greeted as I opened the door...

"Hello Tracy..." he greeted as he came inside. I closed the door and watched him intently as he stood in the middle of the floor. I could tell he was thinking about what he wanted to say...

"Let's sit down." Jermoll followed me to the sofa and we both sat down...

"Am I the only character you did this to?"

"Yes..."

"Why me?"

"You were the best one..."

"I don't understand..."

"In 'Twisted Mary' you started out as a bad guy and then you redeemed yourself..."

"And then you killed me!!"

"You were killed in the line of duty..."

"You still killed me!!"

"I know..."

"You couldn't kill anybody else?!"

"No..."

"Why not?"

"You were one of the main characters..."

"How'd your cousin feel when you told him what you did to me?"

"He took it personal..."

"So you respond to that by killing me again?!"

"Your 1st death had nothing to do with my cousin!!" I laughed...

"So why didn't you leave well enough alone?! Why couldn't you just let me stay dead in 'Twisted Mary?!"

"I wasn't planning on bringing you back from the dead to kill you again but then the pandemic happened..."

"So you brought me back from the dead to kill me again because of COVID?!"

"Yes..."

"WERE YOU HIGH?!" I bust out laughing...

"HELL NO!!" I laughed... "When we were locked down, readers were saying they were tired of reading the same books over and over so I wanted to shock them and make them laugh..."

"So why didn't you bring somebody else back from the dead then?!"

"Because you and Chandler had unfinished business..."

"Unfinished business?!"

"Chandler wasn't just your Sergeant – he was also your friend..."

"That's true – I still don't see why you didn't leave me dead in 'Twisted Mary'..."

"When the zombies started popping up, it gave me the perfect way to bring you back from the dead so you could say good bye..."

"I never wanted to say good bye – I didn't wanna die!!"

"I know you didn't wanna die – but you died – and Chandler never got a chance to say good bye..."

"You brought me back from the dead for Chandler?!"

"Yes..."

"That's what's up – I still didn't wanna die though..."

"I know..." Jermoll sat there for a few moments...

"You should 'a killed Mary too..."

"Why?"

"Cause – if you had killed Mary, you could 'a brought her back from the dead too – and I could 'a got some more pussy..."

"You know what – that's it – I'm done!!" I exclaimed as we both bust out laughing.

CONVERSATION WITH JORDAN FROM

How Far Are You Willing To Go? Murder Is Just The Beginning

"Hello Jordan..." I greeted as I opened the door...

Hello Trenice – I mean Tracy – I can't believe I just did that..." he laughed nervously...

"It's okay – you're not the first..."

"Ummm... okay..."

"That's not what I meant!" I laughed...

"What did you mean?"

"You're not the first person to call me by my character's name..."

"Are you anything like her?"

"Who?"

"Trenice..."

"There's a part of me in all my characters..."

44

"I can't help but see my wife when I look at you..." he said as he looked at our wedding photos..."

"Thank you..."

"I'm literally looking at myself..."

"Let's sit..." I said as I walked over to the sofa and sat down. Jordan sat across from me and opened his suit jacket...

"Did you do this on purpose?" he asked as he pulled out a copy of the first book in the series...

"Yes..."

"I thought so..."

"Now you're the first..."

"Umm... the first what?"

"You're the first character to bring a copy of the book with you..."

"Really? That's surprising – I figured all your characters would bring their books with them..."

"That would've been cool..."

"Hey!" my husband said as he came in...

"Hi Honey..." I greeted...

"Hey Jordan – I'm Gene..." my husband said as he came over to shake Jordan's hand...

"Nice to meet me..." Jordan laughed as he shook my husband's hand...

"It takes some getting used to..." my husband said as he sat down in my seat across from us...

"Do all her male characters look like you as much as I do?"

"No..."

"How are you able to sit across from us and not be jealous?"

"They may look like me but they ain't me..." my husband answered...

"What'd you think of your story?" I asked, shifting the conversation...

"I love the story. I love my wife..."

"I love your story too..."

"Is my wife coming?"

"Not today..."

"Aww... I was hoping I'd see her here..." he sighed...

"You really love her..." my husband said...

"Yes... I do..."

"We have that in common..." my husband said as he smiled...

"I love the way you wrote your songs into the story..."

"Thank you..." we both said in unison and then we all laughed...

"Especially the chapters where Trenice was in the hospital and we gave each other love letters..."

"Yeesss..." I sighed...

"That was a lot..."

"Yes it was..."

"I like my relationship with that detective too..."

"So does he..."

"Really? He's an actual detective?"

"Yes..."

"Does he know what you wrote about us?"

"I gave him a few pages..."

"Oh wow!!" he exclaimed... "Is he the only one you gave a few pages to?"

"Yes..."

"I like the relationships we have with our friends too..."

"So do I..."

"Do you guys have close friends like that?"

"We have a few..." my husband answered...

"That bridal shower was wild!!" Jordan exclaimed...

"I actually turned that into a separate book..."

"You did?!"

"Yes – I wanted to bring the characters to life..."

"Can I see it?!"

"Sure – I'll be right back..." I answered as I got up and went to the library...

"Your wife is something else..." Jordan told my husband...

"She certainly is..." my husband agreed...

"Here you go..." I said as I sat back down and gave Jordan a copy of 'The Bridal Shower'...

"Oh my God – look at us!!" he exclaimed... "Can I keep this?!"

"Yes..."

"I can't wait to show this to my wife!!" he exclaimed as he put it in his suit jacket... "Did you do this with any other chapters in the series?"

"Not yet..."

"I bet you're going to do the same thing with 'Just Ask'!!"

"How'd you know?!" I laughed...

"Because you have to!! That chapter was crazy!!" he laughed...

"We have that in common too..." my husband said...

"Which part?!"

"The part where your wife started praying for you..."

"Right!!" Jordan exclaimed as we all laughed.

CONVERSATION WITH LINA FROM

'Stalked By Magic'

"Hi!" Lina beamed as she threw her arms around my neck and pulled me into a hug...

"Well hello!" I laughed as I hugged her back...

"Why are you laughing?"

"I didn't expect that..."

"You didn't think I'd be happy to see you?" she asked as she went to sit down in my seat... "Do you want me to get up?"

"No..." I answered as I went to sit on the loveseat across from her. I really didn't expect her to sit in my seat, but I understood why she sat there so I just observed her... "Please don't..." I said as she went to pick up my notebook...

"I'm sorry – I didn't mean..."

"Yes you did..." I interrupted... "You don't need to apologize though..."

"I don't need to apologize?"

"No – it's natural for you to be curious..."

"So why can't I read what you wrote then?"

"Because their story isn't any of your business..."

"Fine..." she sighed as she reclined and got comfortable... "So what made you name my husband after your father?"

"That's a question for him to ask..."

"Is he coming?"

"No..."

"It would've been nice to see him..."

"It would be nicer to see you..."

"I'm right here!" she laughed...

"You're sitting here – but you're not here..."

"So where am I then?"

"You're in limbo..."

"I'm in limbo? I don't understand..."

"You're not sure what's going to happen next..."

"How did you know that?"

"I created you..."

"So what happens next?"

"You live..."

"Do I have children?"

"You didn't use any protection..."

"So am I pregnant?!" she exclaimed as she sat up...

"What do you think?"

"I don't know what to think!"

"That's because you're not supposed to think..."

"That doesn't make any sense!"

"You're supposed to enjoy your happy ending..."

"I am – I just want to know what happens next!" she laughed...

"If you were really enjoying your happy ending you wouldn't be asking me what happens next..." Lina sat there for a few moments without speaking. I watched her intently as she searched her mind for her next question...

"Will there be a part 2?"

"No..."

"Whhhyyy???"

"Because you don't need a part 2..."

"So I'm just going to be stuck in limbo indefinitely..." she sighed...

"You're stuck in limbo now – but you don't have to be..."

"How do I get out of limbo if you're not writing a part 2?"

"You listen to the readers..."

"I listen to the readers?"

"Whenever a character has a happy ending the readers predict what happens next..."

"So I live through them..." she sighed as she smiled...

"Exactly..."

"How long do I live?"

"You live as long as readers read and re-read your story..."

"Oh wow..." she whispered as tears came to her eyes...

"Are you okay?" I asked as I stood up and put my hand on her shoulder...

"I'm alive..." she answered as she stood up and pulled me into a hug.

CONVERSATION WITH MARY FROM
'Twisted Mary'

"Hello Mary..." I greeted...

"Hello Tracy..." she greeted as she came inside. I closed the door and she went and sat down on the loveseat...

"Would you like some coffee?"

"No thank you..."

"Okay – let's get started..."

"I've been waiting for this... but now that I'm here..."

"What?"

"I was ready to pop off before I got here!"

"Why?"

"Well – you didn't exactly make me out to be anyone's favorite character..."

"You'd be surprised how many readers love you..."

"Really?!" she snapped sarcastically..."

"I'm serious..."

"What makes you say that?"

"You were the character everyone knew..."

"Oh I gotta hear this!"

"You had an affair with a married man..."

"Thanks to you..." she mumbled...

"Not really. I needed the readers to know where Starr came from and as the story continued, I realized you needed to have your story told..."

"Like I said – thanks to you – my story was told by Bazil & Beautiee..."

"Bazil & Beautiee only knew part of your story..."

"Thanks to you, they knew the worst part..."

"Bazil knew more than Beautiee did..."

"Don't make excuses for Beautiee..."

"I'm surprised at you..." I said as I shook my head...

"You created me and you're surprised?"

"Yes..."

"Why are you surprised by me?"

"I'm surprised that after all this time - you still don't get it..."

"Oh I get it alright – you just don't want to acknowledge what you did to me..."

"You had an affair with Bazil while he was married to Janet..."

"Tell me something I don't know..." she said as she rolled her eyes...

"You had an affair with Bazil while you were in a relationship with Wayne..."

"Is there a point to this trip down memory lane?" she asked as she threw up her hands...

"The point is that is where your story began – but that's not where your story ended...

"Okay – I'll give you that – I was happy when I became a major character..."

"So were the readers..."

"You think so?"

"Absolutely – why do you think I didn't kill you?"

"You couldn't kill me – I laughed when you had Beautiee thinking about it though..."

"You just said you laughed when Beautiee thought about killing you but when you sat down you were ready to pop off because – according to you – I didn't make you out to be anyone's favorite character..."

"So what?"

"So you really think the reason I didn't kill you is because I couldn't kill you?"

"You couldn't kill me if you wanted to – you needed me!!" she laughed...

"Well – I suppose that's one way of looking at it..."

"That's the ONLY way to look at it..."

"I hate to break it to you – that's not true – I'm actually going to enjoy breaking this to you – I didn't kill you because THEY needed you – I didn't need you..." Mary sat there quiet as she was processing what I said...

"YOU FUCKING BITCH!!"

"I know..." I sneered...

"You still can't kill me..." she laughed...

"Never say never..."

"You just said they needed me..."

"The characters that've been killed don't need you anymore..."

"You only killed Jermoll..."

"When's the last time you read your story?"

"It's been a while – why?"

"You need to go re-read it and see..."

"It doesn't matter who's been killed – you still can't kill me – my husband needs me and my daughters need me..."

"And vice-versa..."

"What's that supposed to mean?!" she snapped...

"Do you really need me to spell it out for you?"

"Yes..."

"You love your husband... and Beautiee's husband..."

"I DO NOT LOVE BAZIL!! I HATE THAT MUTHA FUCKA!!"

"You don't hate Bazil – you hate what Bazil did to you..."

"Whatever..."

"You never got over him – and Beautiee knows it..."

"So what?"

"So you need to be careful..."

"Why? We both know you won't kill me..."

"It's one thing for Beautiee to know you never got over Bazil – but if Wayne finds out you never got over Bazil, you'll lose him for good..."

"Bye..." she said as she got up, opened the door, walked out, and closed the door behind her.

CONVERSATION WITH
RASHAD FROM

His Best Friend'

"Hey..." Rashad greeted as I turned around...

"What the hell are you doing here?!"

"Calm down – I'm not here to hurt you... I just wanna talk..."

"I didn't invite you here!"

"If I waited for an invitation, I would've never been invited..."

"You're right..."

"Do you want me to leave?"

"No..."

"Thank you..." he said as he sat down..."

"Why are you here?"

"As I said... I wanna talk to you..."

"You don't wanna talk to me – you need to talk to me..."

"You should know... you created me..."

"Yes... I created you..."

"Why?"

"Why did I create you?"

"That's one question..."

"I needed to..."

"You needed to create a psychotic maniac?"

"Yes..."

"I'm not a psychotic maniac – you didn't have to do that to me!"

"You're not a psychotic maniac – you had a psychotic break – there's a difference..."

"You killed me!"

"I know – I'm sorry..."

"Are you?!"

"Yes..."

"Why'd you do it then?! All I did was get pussy – I never took it – you created me so you know that!"

"Yes – I created you – but I also put a face to the men that get away with it..."

"The men that get away with what?!"

"Men like you – you go from woman to woman to woman – you don't give a damn if she catches feelings or not – as far as you're concerned, she's nothing more than a conquest!"

"Now I get it..."

"Get what?"

"You created me... to get even..."

"No I didn't..."

"Yea right!" he laughed...

"I'm serious..."

"So you're telling me that it never happened to you?"

"Not me..."

"Someone else?"

"All my stories have an element of truth to them..."

"That doesn't answer my question..."

"It wasn't meant to..."

"Why'd you kill me?"

"I had to kill you..."

"You had to?! Why?!"

"Are you seriously asking me that after what you did to Clarisse?"

"You could've had me arrested! You could've had Randall bust me down to the white meat!"

"I could've written it that way – and Clarisse would've lost Randall – and you would've continued to be an arrogant, cocky, narcissistic muthafucka that would've lost a friend – both of you would've lost a business – and instead of taking accountability for your actions, you would've blamed Randall for it all and moved on to your next conquest..."

"I never thought of it like that..."

"Clarisse didn't deserve that..."

"No she didn't..."

"Randall was a good man..."

"I know, I know!" he laughed...

"He deserved to be happy..."

"Yea... he did..."

"Are you still mad at me?"

"Naa... I get it..."

"Good..."

"Aiight – I won't keep you – I got things to do..." he said as he got up...

"You're dead!" I laughed...

"So is Helen..." he said as he smiled a sinister smile...

"Oh my God – are you serious?"

"You already know... you created me..." he laughed as he disappeared.

CONVERSATION WITH
SEAN FROM
'The Ultimate Con'

"Hello Beautiee..." Sean greeted as he walked in...

"Please call me Tracy..." I said as we both sat on the loveseat...

"Why can't I call you Beautiee?"

"Because Tracy is the author..."

"You mean Tracy is the serial killer..."

"Yes... I am..."

"Why'd you kill me?"

"It was necessary..."

"You could've let me live!" he snapped...

"Watch your tone Sean..."

"Or what?! You'll kill me again?!" he laughed...

"If you don't watch your tone I'll write a part 3 and make sure Bazil discovers you weren't his friend at all – he'll discover you were nothing but a con – the readers will realize the ultimate con wasn't committed by Snow and Flick – it was actually committed by you..."

"That's fucked up..."

"I'm glad we have an understanding..."

"You could've at least let me get some pussy..."

"You got pussy from your wife..."

"I deserved more than beating off in the shower..."

"Are you mad because you got conned, are you mad because you didn't get any pussy, or are you mad because you were killed?"

"I'm mad at all of it – I get that I had to be conned – but I died without gettin' the pussy – you had her husband kill me – I should 'a got the pussy!" I immediately bust out laughing... "What the fuck are you laughing at?!" he snapped...

"You're not mad because you didn't get the pussy – you're mad because you fell for Snow!" I laughed...

"Of course I fell for Snow! And you killed me before I had a chance to win her heart!"

"You never had a chance..."

"I would've had a chance if you had killed Flick instead of me..."

"You're delusional..." I laughed again. Sean wasn't smiling. I could see the anger in his eyes...

"Don't call me delusional..."

"Okay – you're not delusional – you fell for Snow – her husband dies instead of you – you profess your love for her – she falls into your arms, she apologizes for conning you – she promises to give you back your money, you tell her you forgive her, you leave your wife, and you both live happily ever after..."

"Alright – you've made your point..."

"What made you see my point?"

"I'd never forgive them for conning me..."

"And?"

"I'd be consumed with revenge..."

And?"

"I would've wound up dead anyway because my wife would've killed me..."

"Exactly." Sean sat there quiet. I watched him intently as he searched his mind before asking me another question...

"What if I am delusional?"

"What?"

"If you wrote a part 3 and I forgive Snow – after I kill her husband of course – would I get some pussy before my wife kills me?"

"Oh my God!" I exclaimed and then I bust out laughing...

"Can't blame me for trying!" he laughed as he got up to leave. We both continued laughing as he opened the door, left, and closed the door behind him.

CONVERSATION WITH SONIA FROM

'Twisted Beautiee'

"Hello Tracy..." Sonia greeted as I opened the door...

"Hello Sonia – come in." Sonia came inside and stopped to look at our wedding photos...

"Hmmm..."

"I guess you see the resemblance..."

"That's not all I see..."

"What else do you see?"

"I see how beautiful you are..." she breathed as she stepped closer to me, pushed my hair behind my ear, and tried to kiss me...

"Stop..." I said as I stepped back from her...

"I'm sorry – I didn't mean to offend you – I thought..."

"You thought I was Beautiee..." I interrupted...

"Yes... and no..."

"What's that supposed to mean?"

"I don't want to upset you..."

"If you don't tell me what's on your mind, we won't be able to have a conversation..."

"Are you sure you want me to answer your question?"

"C'mon – let's go sit on the loveseat..." I answered as I walked over to the loveseat and she followed. We both sat down, turned to face each other, and then she spoke...

"I didn't think I'd ever hear from you after you killed me..."

"I get that..."

"When you invited me over... ummm..."

"What?"

"I started fantasizing about us..."

"Hmmm..."

"What does that mean?"

"You're the first..."

"I'm the first woman?"

"You're the first character to fantasize about me after I killed them..."

"Ooohhh..."

"Is that what you wanted to tell me?"

"I'm in love!" she blurted out...

"Yes - I know – you fell in love with Beautiee..."

"I think I'm in love with you..." she said as she took my hand...

"Sonia – you're not in love with me..."

"Please don't try to dismiss my feelings..."

"I'm not dismissing your feelings – I understand your feelings..."

"You just told me I'm not in love with you..."

"You fell in love with Beautiee – a character I created – and you love me because I created you both and I gave you the love of your life..."

"So you agree with me then..."

"You love me – but you're in love with Beautiee..."

"I wanted Bazil to die..."

"I know..."

"If Bazil died, Beautiee would've turned to me for comfort..."

"Beautiee never would've turned to you..."

"What makes you say that?"

"You're responsible for the man in the closet..."

"Trevor..."

"You didn't really think that through..."

"That's your fault..."

"You and Trevor were consumed with revenge – you wanted Bazil dead because you wanted Beautiee – Trevor wanted Bazil dead because Bazil rejected him – neither one of you thought about what would happen once Beautiee found out you were in on the plan from the beginning..." Sonia sat there quiet for a few moments, processing what I said...

"Damn – that Bitch would've killed us both..."

"Exactly..."

"And she would've gotten away with it..."

"Exactly..."

"Why'd she have to turn me out?" she laughed...

"Because she was the one you fell in love with..."

"Can I ask you a personal question?"

"Sure..."

"Did I make you uncomfortable when I told you I fantasized about you?"

"Nope..."

"Really?"

"Naa – you're not the first character to tell me they love me..."

"Oh my God – you are so full of yourself!" she laughed...

"Do you see Trevor?"

"All the time..."

"How is he?"

"He's mad at you..."

"I'm sorry – he had to die..."

"That's not why he's mad at you..."

"Really? Why's he mad at me then?"

"It's stupid..."

"Tell me!"

"He's mad because you didn't bring us back from the dead in 'Erotic Zombies!'"

"Oh my God!" I laughed... "Wait – I can't!"

"I know – it's crazy!" she laughed... "When he told me that, I imagined our bones intertwining and breaking as we changed positions!" she laughed again. Sonia noticed I wasn't laughing. She watched my facial expression change immediately... "Are you okay?"

"Trevor isn't mad at me because I didn't bring you back from the dead in 'Erotic Zombies' to fuck..."

"I don't understand..."

"He's mad at me because I didn't give him another chance to try and kill Bazil..."

"Oh my God... are you sure about that?"

"Oh yea..."

"I shouldn't've told you..."

"Don't worry about it..." I sighed...

"I guess I should get going..." she sighed...

"Okay..." I said as I stood up and went towards the door...

"Will I see you again?" she asked as she came towards me..."

"No..." I answered as I opened the door...

"I'm glad I was your first..." she said as she pulled me into a hug..."

"I'll never forget it..." I laughed...

"Good bye Tracy..." she said as she let go of me and went outside...

"Good bye Sonia..."

"I'll tell Trevor you said hello..."

"Oh no the hell I didn't!" I exclaimed as she walked down the street. I closed the door and went to sit on the loveseat... "Thank you Sonia..." I said out loud as I smiled mischievously and started thinking about 'Erotic Zombies In The U.K.'

CONVERSATION WITH STARR FROM

'Twisted Starr'

"Hi Starr..." I greeted...

"Hello Tracy..." she greeted as she came inside. She looked around and then she stopped to look at our wedding photos... "Niagara Falls..." she sighed...

"Yea..."

"Now I see why you wrote about Niagara Falls in our story..." she said as she went to sit down on the loveseat. I sat down beside her and we looked at each other for a few moments...

"Oh she's here – hello Starr..." my husband greeted as he came inside... "I'm Gene..."

"You look like my grandfather..."

"And you look prettier in person..."

"Aww... thank you..."

"You're welcome..."

"My husband saw you first..." I said...

"I thought you saw me first?"

"I saw your cover first – but my husband saw you in the commercials first..."

"You've seen my commercials?!" she exclaimed as she sat up...

"Yes..." we both answered as my husband sat down on the sofa across from us...

"We saw your grandfather's commercials too..." I said...

"Really?! Do all your characters do commercials?!"

"So far we've only seen you and your grandfather..." I answered...

"What made you decide to give me my own story?"

"You were gone for 18 years. You went through a lot. I thought it was important to tell your story..."

"You did the same thing with my mother..."

"Yes I did..."

"I feel like I should call you Mom..."

"Aww... that's sweet..."

"Well – you are my parents – you created me – you created all of us..."

"That's true – but I can't look at your grandfather as our child..." I laughed...

"I can see where that would be weird..." she laughed...

"So do you like how everything turned out?"

"I love my story..." she sighed...

"I'm glad...

"I love the way you wrote about us in 'Twisted Christmas'..."

"That's one of my favorite books in the Twisted Series..."

"I had my Moms, my Dads, my Husband, my Brothers, my Sister, my Babies, and my new best friends – I hope we do every Christmas like that every year..."

"You will..."

"Does that mean our story isn't over?"

"Well... technically your story will never be over..."

"Really?!" she exclaimed as she sat up...

"The way I wrote your story, all the children were together – the readers will talk about the children, they'll wonder how they're doing in school, etc. – plus, I'm sure you've read 'Erotic Zombies'..."

"Yes! That story was crazy!"

"Did you like it?"

"I loved it!!" she laughed...

"The good thing about you being married to Chandler is that you'll follow him wherever he goes..."

"Wherever he goes?"

"Yes – he's a Sergeant so he shows up at crime scenes and investigations where I've killed other characters..."

"And he always comes home to me..." she sighed...

"Yes he does..."

"Will my mother follow me too?"

"Not necessarily..."

"Is that because Beautiee doesn't like her?"

"No – it's because your mother lives in Canada with Wayne. You were all birthed from the Twisted Series – your husband is one of the main characters because of the murders that take place and the majority of my stories take place in Fairfield & Westchester counties..."

"Are you ever going to kill my mother?" she asked with concern in her voice...

"Starr..." I said as I took her hand and held it... "I'm not going to kill your mother..."

"Okay..." she sighed as she smiled and stood up...

"Leaving so soon?" my husband asked...

"Yea – I need to get back to my babies..."

"I'm glad we got to meet you..." my husband said as he stood up...

"I'm glad I got to meet you too..." she said as she pulled my husband into a hug...

"Kiss your babies for me..." I said as I pulled her into a hug...

"I will..." she said as she opened the door to leave and we all went outside... "Bye!" she said as she waived and we watched her walk down the street.

CONVERSATION WITH STERLING FROM

Thirst Quencher

"Hey My Thirst Quencher!!" I squealed as I opened the door...

"Hello Tracy..." he greeted...

"Let's go outside – I've got Henny on deck!!"

"Okay!!" he exclaimed as he followed me outside...

"Hello Sterling, I'm Gene..." my husband greeted as he extended his hand...

"Nice to meet you – am I the only one drinkin'?"

"I'm having Henny too – I just have more ice..." I answered as I held up my cup with the straw...

"Damn! How much Henny you have in that cup?!"

"I have enough to make sure I don't need another drink..." I laughed...

"I'm just sippin' on ice tea..." my husband added...

"Okay..." Sterling started to say. When he paused to take a sip I knew we'd be turning up... "First of all – thank you for Lexi..."

"You're welcome..."

"Second – where are the women that are willing to put up with their man being an escort?" he laughed...

"It's not that she was willing to put up with you being an escort – it's more that she knew who you were and she wanted you in spite of it..."

"I couldn't believe she asked me to marry her..."

"My readers thought that was crazy..."

"I thought it was crazy!"

"Well... good dick has been known to drive a woman crazy..." I said as I took a sip of my drink. Sterling looked at me, looked at my husband, and smiled to himself...

"I didn't think Lexi was crazy – she fell in love with me – the crazy one was LaShonda!!" he exclaimed as we all bust out laughing... "And the way you described her – Hood Ratchet, Ghetto, Titty Saggin' Breath Stinkin' – I was like damn – why I gotta fuck her?!" We were laughing so hard we were holding our stomachs...

"Every time I re-read that I say damn — I can't believe I wrote this!!" I exclaimed as we continued laughing...

"I was scared when I found out she went to school with Lexi — I thought you were gonna have Lexi kill her..."

"Naa... that would've been easy and predictable..."

"One thing your readers know about you is your characters are not predictable..."

"Exactly..."

"Especially when Lexi knocks her down off her pedestal..."

"I enjoyed taking her down..."

"I could tell!!" he exclaimed as we all laughed... "And the way I fucked my clients' good bye!!" he laughed...

"That was crazy!!" I laughed...

"I don't know what's crazier — me fucking them goodbye or her waiting and crossing them off the list!!" he exclaimed as we all bust out laughing again...

"I had so much fun writing that..."

"So what happens with me and Lexi?"

"I can't tell you..."

"Oh my God — is she gonna die?!"

"Would I do that to you?"

"Well..."

"I'm not going to kill Lexi..."

"So our story isn't over?"

"Your story isn't over..."

"Do we live happily ever after?"

"Let's just say you live..."

"Oh damn – I guess I better brace myself..."

"Yes..."

"Aiight – I'ma go now..." he said as he stood up...

"You alright?" my husband asked...

"Yea..." he sighed...

"C'mon – I'll walk you to the front..." my husband said as he got up and Sterling followed him down the driveway and I went back in the house...

"You're gonna be alright..." my husband said...

"You sure?" Sterling asked...

"Yea..."

"How can you be so sure?"

"Because I know how your story ends..."

"How does it end?"

"I'm sworn to secrecy..."

"Oh well – I tried – at least I know we'll be alright..." he said as he walked down the street and my husband came back into the house.

CONVERSATION WITH
TRENICE FROM

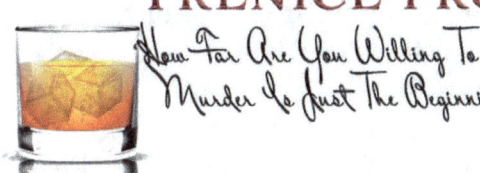

How Far Are You Willing To Go?
Murder Is Just The Beginning

"Hi Trenice..." I greeted as I opened the door...

"Hey..." she sighed as she came in, went towards the loveseat, and sat down...

"What's wrong?"

"I don't know where to start..." she sighed...

"Start at the beginning..."

"I went through a lot of shit..."

"Yes you did..."

"I can't believe I'm sitting here talking to you like we're friends..." I was taken aback by that. I had to compose myself before I responded...

"Are we enemies?"

"No – but if I'm being honest – I'm upset with you..."

"I know..."

"You do?"

"Of course I do..."

"That actually makes me feel a little better..."

"I'm glad..."

"Did you plot me out in advance?"

"I didn't plot you out in advance, but I knew where I was going with your story..."

"Was it hard to write sometimes?"

"Absolutely..."

"Why'd you write it then?"

"Because some people don't need therapy, support groups, or medication – some people need heroes..."

"Aww..." Trenice started crying and I pulled her into a hug... "You did turn me into a bad Bitch..."

"Not really – I just showed the readers what you were made of..."

"Yea – I'm a bad Bitch!" she laughed...

"That's not all you are..."

"I can't believe how things turned out..."

"I can..."

"Of course you can – you wrote it!!"

"Yes I did..."

"Thank you for giving us a baby..."

"You're welcome..."

"I was worried you were going to write that we couldn't have children..."

"Nope..."

"Thank you for giving Jordan a copy of 'The Bridal Shower' – I love it..."

"You're welcome..."

"Can we have a copy of 'Just Ask' too?"

"Sure..."

"Are you going to write any other spin-offs?"

"I've thought about it..."

"Really?! Do we have more kids?!" she exclaimed as she sat up...

"I haven't thought about that..."

"Have you thought about who'd be in the spin-off?"

"I'm not sure..."

"Okay – I'll stop asking questions - wait – I have one more question..."

"Yes Trenice?"

"Am I ever going to die?"

"Why the hell would you ask me that?!"

"Well... you like to kill people!!" she laughed...

"I'm not going to kill you... yet..."

"Oh my God!!"

"I'm just playing!!" I laughed...

"That wasn't funny!!" she laughed...

"Why are you laughing then?"

"Okay – it was kinda funny – but it's not funny..."

"I'm not going to kill you Trenice..."

"Are you going to kill my husband?"

"I'm not going to kill your husband – and I'm not going to answer any more questions..."

"Are you mad at me?"

"That's not going to work..."

"I love how you wrote your songs into our story..."

"So do I..."

"The song on our wedding day was my favorite..."

"Your wedding is my favorite wedding..."

"Aww..."

"You got married on our wedding day..."

"Was your wedding anything like ours?"

"Yea..." I sighed as I smiled. Trenice smiled at me and watched me for a few moments...

"I better get going..." she said as she stood up...

"Okay..." I said as I stood up and pulled her into a hug...

"I'm glad we got a chance to talk..."

"So am I..."

"Are you feeling better?"

"Of course I'm feeling better – I'm a hero..." she answered as she went out the door.

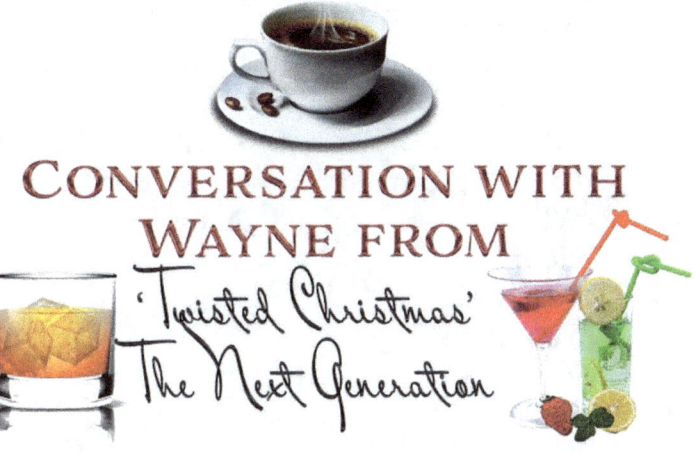

CONVERSATION WITH WAYNE FROM

'Twisted Christmas'
The Next Generation

"Hello Wayne..." I greeted as I opened the door...

"Hello Tracy..." he greeted as he came inside...

"Is it okay if I sit here?" he asked as he went towards my husband's seat...

"Sure." Wayne sat down and looked around...

"You sure you don't want to sit on the sofa? You might be more comfortable...

"I'd prefer to sit by the door..." he responded nervously...

"C'mon – come sit on the sofa with me – I won't bite..." I laughed...

"Okay..." he said as he got up and followed me over to the sofa... "So how does this work?" he asked as we sat down...

"We're just going to talk..."

"About me?"

"Yes — unless you wanna talk about someone else..."

"I do..."

"Okay – go ahead..."

"When I first started reading my story, I didn't like it..."

"I know..."

"You know?"

"Yes — you lost the love of your life to prison and another man..."

"That's not all I lost..."

"I know..."

"I thought when I came back into her life, I'd be welcomed with open arms – but I wasn't..."

"That would've been a different story..."

"I wanted that story until I continued reading..."

"You wanted to know what was going to happen next..."

"I went through a lot..."

"You all went through a lot..."

"I was surprised you didn't write me walking away and never coming back..."

"Your story started with you coming back from walking away..."

"I loved the way you used Beautiee to bring me back..."

"I loved that too..."

"I wasn't sure what was going to happen when I caught Mary with Jermoll..." he laughed...

"I had a lot of fun with that..."

"You had a little too much fun!" he laughed...

"You mean you had a little too much fun!" I laughed...

"I thought you were gonna have me kill her but you did the opposite – for a while anyway..."

"I gave you the wife you always wanted..."

"At first I thought she didn't want me..."

"She wanted you – but you left so she thought you didn't want her anymore..."

"I understand that – but she wasn't over Bazil..."

"That's true..."

"Thank you for acknowledging that..."

"I had to acknowledge that – it's a big part of your story..."

"It's still a big part of our story..."

"Your story changed for the better..."

"After we went through a lot more..."

"You didn't think you'd ever get there – did you?"

"No..." he laughed...

"I started to end your story after you moved to Canada – but Bazil was intrigued..."

"He thought we had his money..."

"Yes..."

"I started to think it was over for us until you wrote 'Twisted Mary 2 & 3'..."

"I couldn't help it! I had to finish it!"

"You went above and beyond when you had us praying and talking to God..."

"Thank you..."

"I loved that we were both praying for the same thing without realizing it..."

"As sad as that was, that was my favorite part..."

"I didn't think we'd make it..."

"I never wanted to kill you..."

"Gee – thanks!"

"You're welcome!" I exclaimed as we both laughed...

"I love how you brought us all together in 'Twisted Christmas'..."

"I had so much fun writing that story..."

"Every time I look at the cover and see my daughter Sky I tear up..." he sniffed...

"Aww..."

"I'm sorry..." he sniffed as he took a handkerchief from his pocket and blew his nose...

"You don't need to apologize – I'm glad you're finally happy..."

"I have everything I ever wanted..."

"Are you sure?"

"Oh God – what?!"

"Relax Wayne – I was thinking you might want another baby!"

"Oh wow – now that you mention it – a son would be nice – unless Mary doesn't..."

"Mary was here the other day..." I purposely interrupted...

"I know..." he sighed...

"What's wrong?"

"She thinks you're going to kill her..."

"Why would I do that?! Haven't you been through enough?!"

"That's what I said!!"

"Starr was here too..."

"Really?!"

"Yes..."

"Was she happy to see you?!"

"Yes – she said my husband looks like her grandfather..."

"Well – now that you mention it..." he said as he leaned forward to look at our wedding photos... "Your husband does look like her grandfather..."

"Have you seen their commercials?"

"They have commercials?!"

"Yes..."

"How did you get lucky enough to pick two characters that have commercials in real life?"

"I have no idea – but I'm sure glad it happened..."

"Well I guess I'll get going..." he said as he stood up...

"Okay..." I said as I stood up too...

"Thank you..." he sighed as he pulled me into a hug...

"You're welcome Wayne..." I said as I hugged him back. After we let go of each other, I walked him to the door...

"I'll see you soon..." he said before he opened the door and then he left, closing the door behind him.